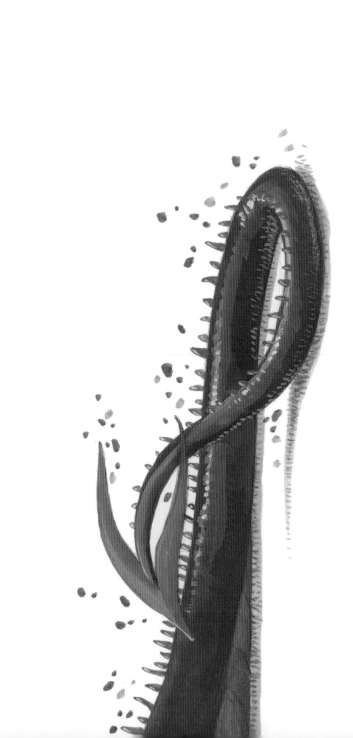

SIMON AND THE BIG, BAD, ANGRY BEASTS

A Book about Anger

To Charlotte, the best of mothers,
who shares with me the anger of our
children and, of course, all the joys

SIMON AND THE BIG, BAD, ANGRY BEASTS

A Book about Anger

Ian De Haes

Flyaway books

Louisville, Kentucky

The first time Simon got mad,

it was after he had caused a lot of mischief.

His father had punished him, and Simon was angry with the whole world.

He was so mad that he had a big temper tantrum.

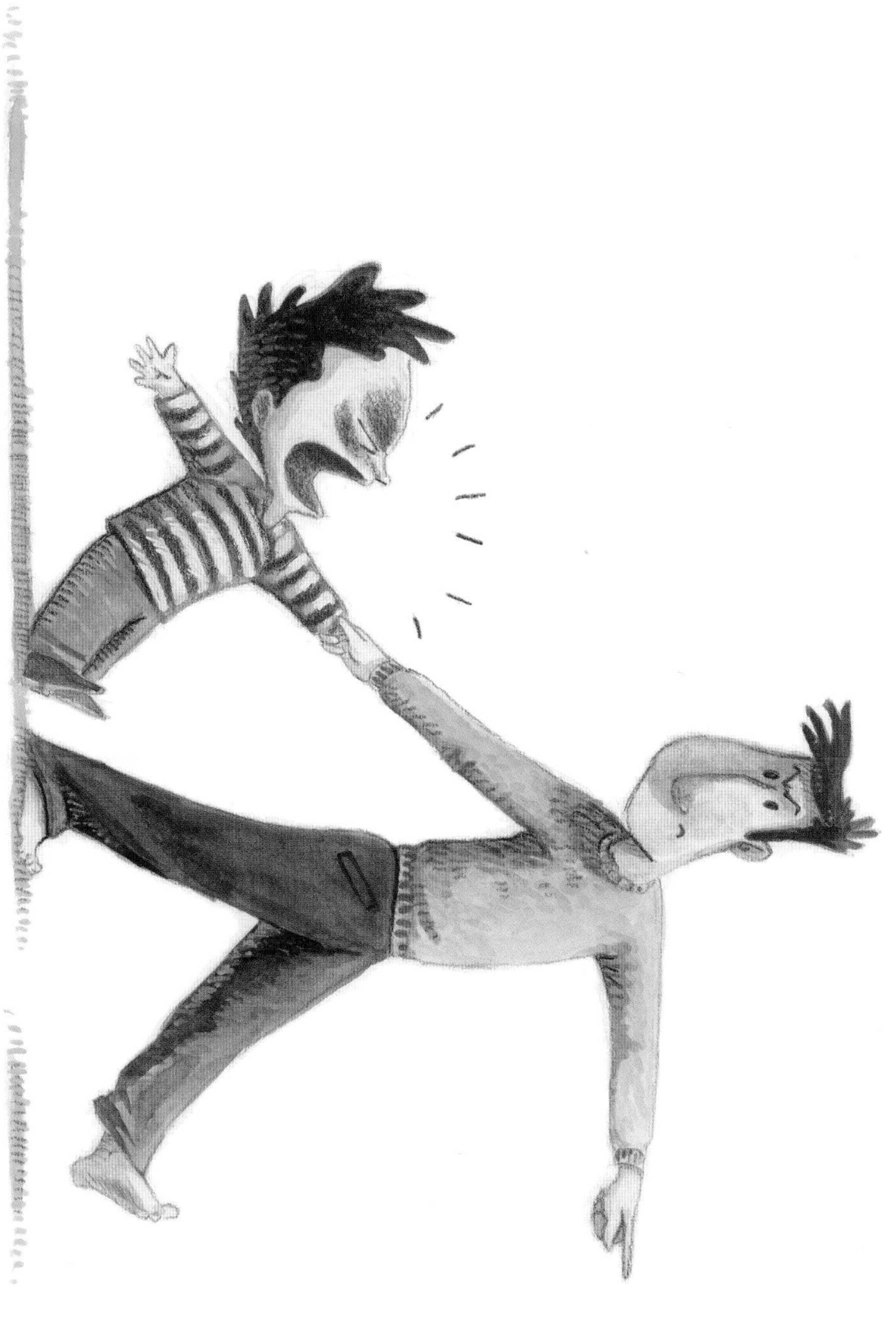

I n his room, where his father had sent him,
Simon banged noisily on the door.
Suddenly he discovered that a big ram was
pounding the door along with him!

It was great, it was marvelous, it was magical to have

a ram that charged after anything that made Simon mad.

If Simon's father asked him for something, bam!

The animal knocked him down.

The second time Simon got really mad,

he had just lost at a game and didn't think it was fair.

Suddenly, to his absolute amazement,

he saw that his ram had transformed into an alligator.

It was great, it was marvelous, it was magical to have a not-so-nice alligator that snapped at people with his teeth when Simon wasn't happy.

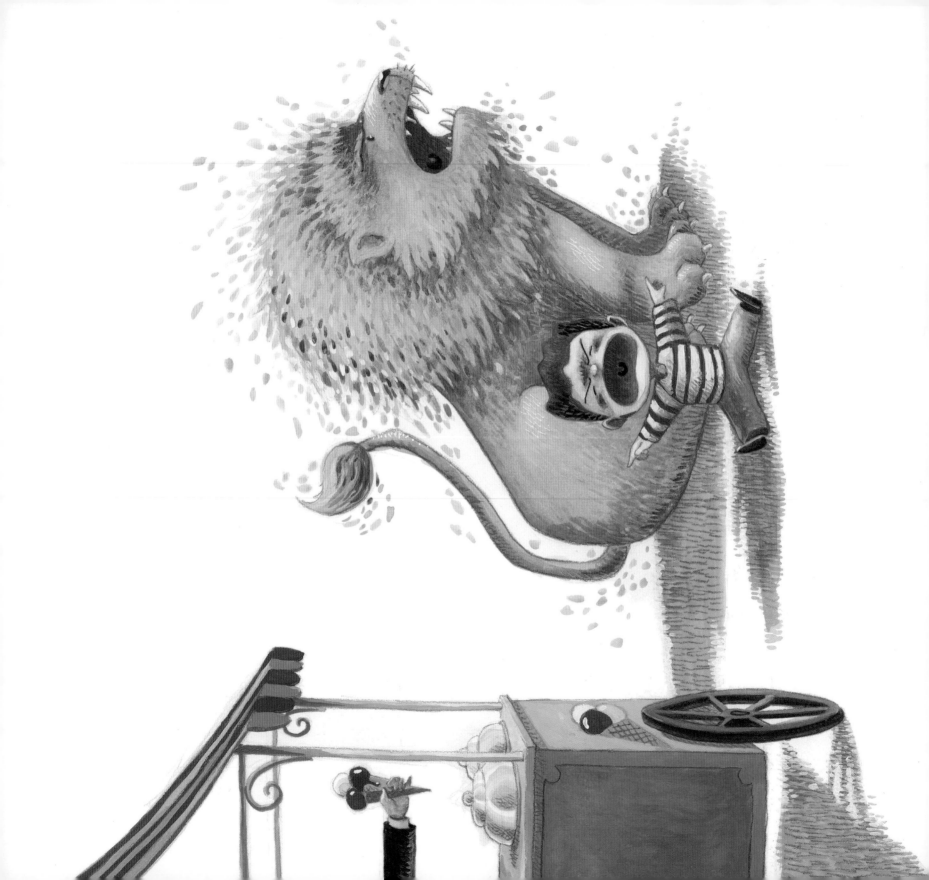

The third time he got very angry,
it was because his mother had told him no.

Suddenly his alligator transformed
into a terrifying lion!

It was great, it was marvelous, it was magical to have a great African lion by his side.

No one dared refuse him anything!

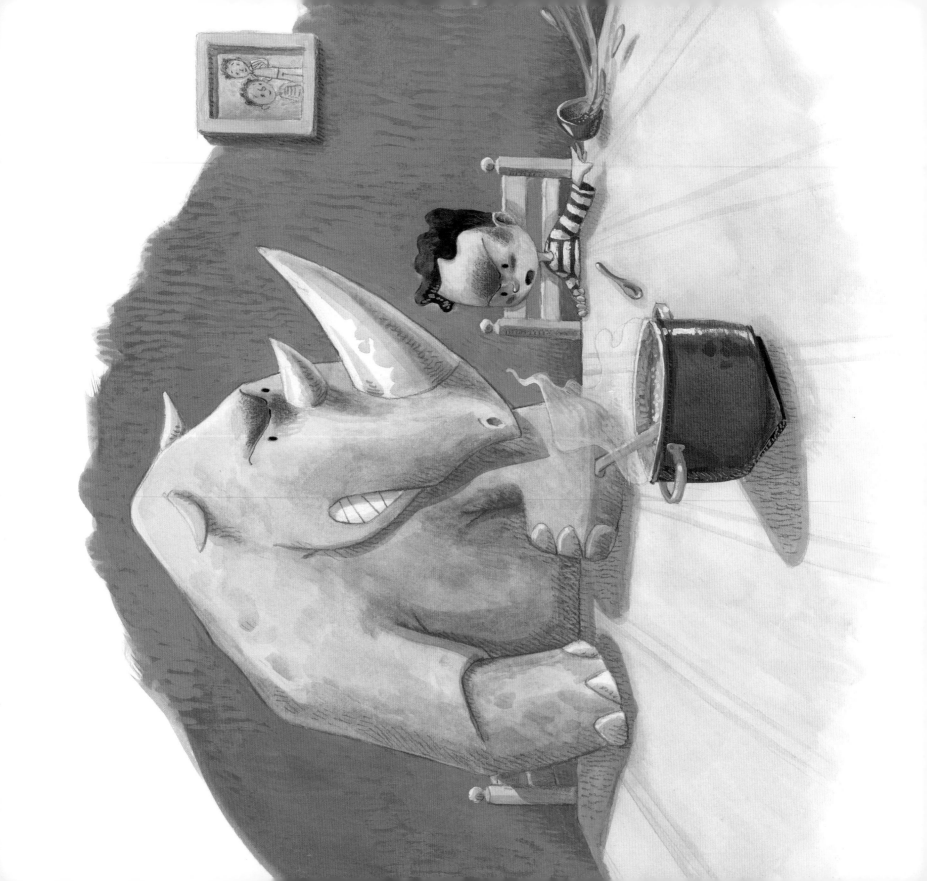

The fourth time Simon got angry, he flew into a rage because he had been forced to eat all his soup! He saw that his big lion had become an enormous rhinoceros!

It was great, it was marvelous, it was magical

to have a fearsome rhinoceros at his service.

Everyone ran away as soon

as he sat down at the dinner table!

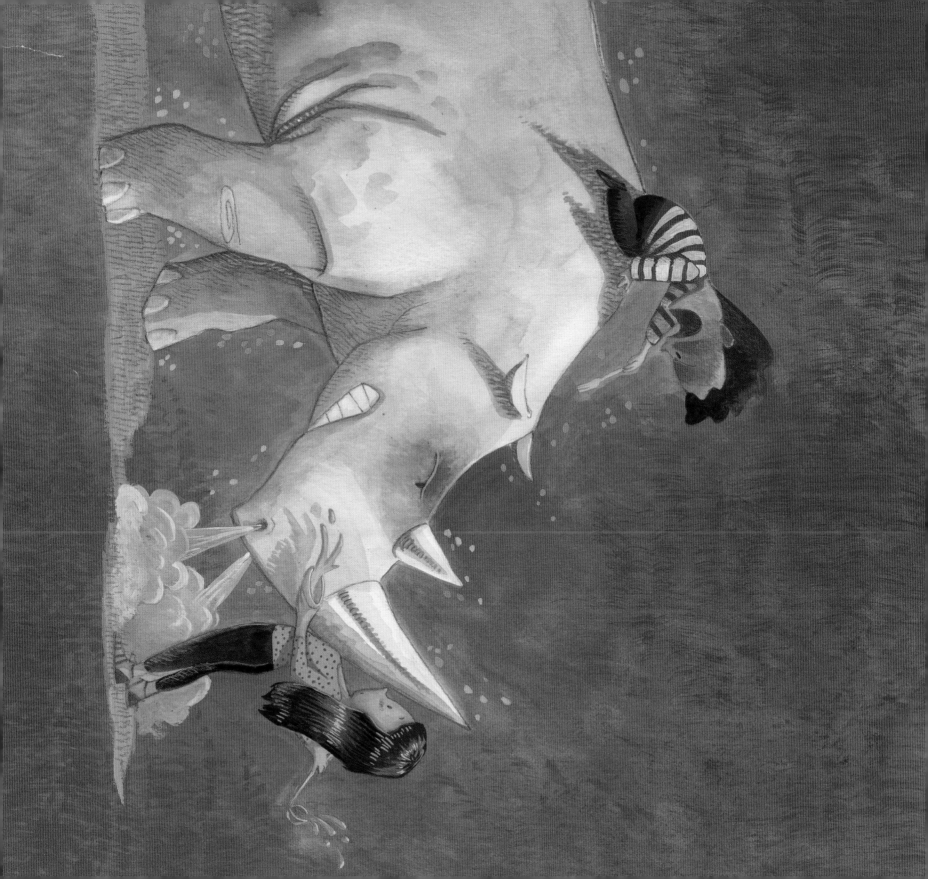

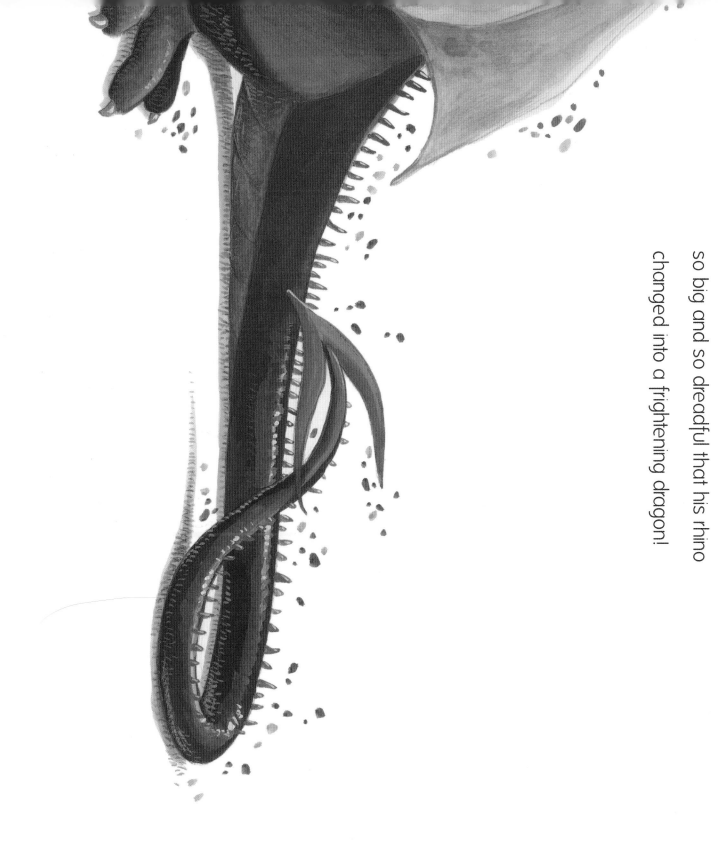

hen one day, Simon's anger
burst out without a reason. It was
so big and so dreadful that his rhino
changed into a frightening dragon!

It was great, it was marvelous, it was magical to have a dragon that spit flames and sent everyone running. They began calling him "Simon the Terrible."

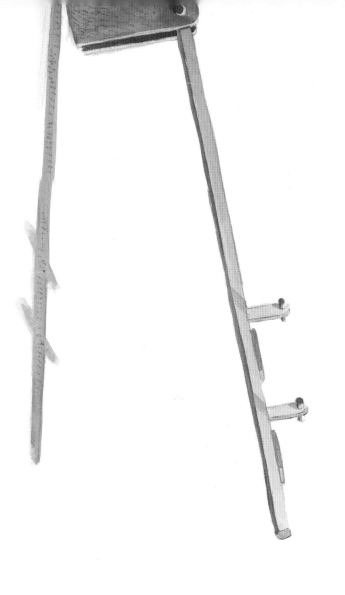

*B*ut then he realized that his parents, his pals, his best friend . . . none of them wanted to play with him anymore. Suddenly, he felt quite lonely.

I t was not so great, not so marvelous, not so magical to always have such anger. He would have preferred to get a hug from his dad or a kiss from his mom or to play with his friends like before.

Ian De Haes is a Belgian artist and painter who illustrates picture books. Learn more at his website http://iandehaes.com/.

Library of Congress Cataloging-in-Publication Data
Names: De Haes, Ian, author, illustrator.
Title: Simon and the big, bad, angry beasts : a book about anger / Ian De Haes.
Other titles: Coleres de Simon. English
Description: Louisville, KY : Flyaway Books, 2017. | Originally published: Bruxelles, Belgium : Alice Editions, 2016 under the title Les coleres de Simon. | Summary: Whenever Simon gets angry, wild beasts appear to help scare off those who upset him, but he becomes lonely, calms himself, and conjures a new kind of animal friend.
Identifiers: LCCN 2017047281 | ISBN 9780664263553 (hbk : alk. paper)
Subjects: | CYAC: Anger--Fiction. | Animals--Fiction. | Behavior--Fiction.
Classification: LCC PZ7.1.D45 Sim 2017 | DDC [E]--dc23 LC record available at https://lccn.loc.gov/2017047281

PRINTED IN CHINA

Most Flyaway Books are available at special quantity discounts when purchased in bulk by corporations, organizations, and special-interest groups. For more information, please e-mail SpecialSales@flyawaybooks.com.

NOTES

1. Hedda Sharapan, *What Do You Do with the Mad That You Feel? Activity Book to Help Children Manage Anger* (Pittsburg: Family Communications, Inc., 2006), 5.

2. Ibid., 7.

3. Ibid., 5.

4. Dawn Gluskin, "Teaching Children Meditation and Mindfulness," *The Blog, Huffington Post*, September 17, 2013, http://www.huffingtonpost.com/dawn-gluskin/teaching-children-meditat_b_3891216.html.

- In advance, cut out construction paper butterflies in a variety of colors. Call attention to the last pages of the book, in which Simon concentrated until he began to feel calm and then felt as if his dragon had exploded into a thousand butterflies, each one carrying a little piece of his anger away. Encourage the children to choose one or more butterflies and to print on each butterfly a phrase or two describing some situation or circumstance that makes them angry. Have children glue their butterflies to a large sheet of mural paper. Then have them choose other butterflies and print on each one a phrase or two describing how they feel when they are able to let go of their anger. They can glue these butterflies to another sheet of mural paper.

- Distribute drawing materials. Remind the group that when Simon tried to shout away his anger, that only brought out worse creatures than the ones he had imagined before. Invite children to imagine what one of those creatures might look like and to create a picture of it.

- Consider blocking out time for children to engage in mindfulness. See "Teaching Children Mindfulness" for some beginning simple instructions.

TEACHING CHILDREN MINDFULNESS

1. In her blog "Teaching Children Meditation and Mindfulness,"[4] Dawn Gluskin suggests introducing mindfulness using an activity she gleaned from the book *Peaceful Piggy* by Kerry Maclean. Put a little sand or a small amount of glitter in the bottom of a small jar. Fill the jar with water. Shake it up and show the children how the sand or glitter swirls around. Tell the children that the grains of sand or bits of glitter are like the thoughts and feelings that swirl around in our minds. Then put the jar down and let the particles settle. Point out that the sand or glitter is still there, but the water is clearer and more calm. This is how mindfulness can affect your brain and the way you think and feel.

2. Invite children to find a comfortable position for sitting. Set a timer for a short period of time—three to five minutes is probably enough. Suggest that they close their eyes (although this is not essential).

3. Ask them to begin to notice their breathing. After a few moments, encourage them to inhale slowly and deeply. Point out that they will notice their bellies rising on the inhale and lowering on the exhale. Dawn Gluskin suggests that you may want to invite children to clasp their hands together, raising their index fingers and holding them in front of their mouths. Have them inhale slowly, and then as they exhale, they should imagine they are blowing out a birthday candle.

4. After a few moments of deep breathing, you may want to remind them of the butterflies that carried Simon's anger away. Children may want to imagine butterflies carrying away bits of negative emotions they may be having.

5. When the timer signals the end of the time of meditation, some children may want to talk about the experience. Acknowledge that sometimes it is hard to settle into silence and that often thoughts may wander or they may feel fidgety. This is perfectly normal! Point out that practice helps people to meditate more effectively.

- Simon didn't know what to do to get rid of his anger. He tried shouting at it to make it go away, but that only brought out worse creatures. If you could imagine worse creatures than a frightening dragon, what would they be? What would they look like, and what would they do?

- Have you ever just gotten mad about nothing? What did you do? How did it make you feel when you couldn't control the way you were feeling? Did it feel great, marvelous, and magical, or did you feel differently? Why?

3. Point out that after a few moments of sitting quietly, Simon felt as if his dragon had exploded into a thousand butterflies, each one carrying a little piece of his anger away. If you think it may be helpful, introduce your child to the process of mindfulness meditation to help deal with anger. Keep in mind that the best way to encourage children to meditate is to model meditating yourself. There are many helpful resources online to guide you as you begin to meditate. See also "Teaching Children Mindfulness" later in this guide.

USING THIS BOOK WITH A GROUP

Teachers and leaders may find the following suggestions helpful in guiding a discussion with a group of children. Just as a good teacher does in any other learning situation, tailor the questions you ask to the particular children in the group, and let their questions and comments shape how the conversation goes.

1. Before reading the book, ask children to name situations in which they have been angry. Ask: What made you mad? How did you show how mad you were? What happened? Then tell them that you are going to read a book about some times when a boy named Simon got very mad, what he did, and what happened. Read the book aloud, stopping to show the illustrations.

2. After reading the book, go through the book again, asking children to look carefully at each illustration and then tell exactly what was happening in each episode that made Simon angry. Recall that after each situation where Simon was angry, we hear that Simon thought "it was great, it was marvelous, it was magical" to have a ferocious animal to scare the people he was mad at.

3. Ask children how they think Simon felt when he suddenly got angry for no reason. Then ask: What if you had been Simon's mother or father, or one of his friends? How do you think you would have felt when Simon's anger got the best of him?

FOLLOW-UP ACTIVITIES

- Give children play dough and suggest that they experiment with shaping it, folding it, and pounding it to see how they might work through strong emotional responses. Or let them choose a color of finger paint that they think expresses anger for them, and encourage them to make patterns. Following these activities, invite children who want to do so to tell why they made the shapes they created or what they think the colors and patterns they made with finger paint say about anger.

need to let the child know you are angry and then walk away for a few moments until you feel more in control. If you have expressed yourself with a certain amount of yelling, you may need to apologize—not for being angry but for raising your voice. A child is helped when an adult acknowledges that adults too can be angry and act in less than helpful ways.

- **Help Children Develop Self-Control.** The late Fred Rogers of *Mister Rogers' Neighborhood* always emphasized that being angry is no excuse for destroying anything or for hurting another person. An angry child who is hitting, kicking, or biting may find it difficult to stop if he or she has not yet developed the language to express those feelings or learned strategies that can help them cope with what they are feeling. For younger children, it may also be quite frightening to be out of control. Family Communications, Inc., the organization created by Rogers, suggests the following basic ways to help children develop self-control:

    - build nurturing, caring relationships;

    - give children clear, simple rules and limits that they can understand;

    - use kindness and firmness to help them stop when they are out of control; and

    - encourage activities to strengthen skills that children need for self-control.[2]

- **Redirect Anger-Induced Behavior.** Strategies teachers and parents used in the past to redirect children's anger, such as hitting a pillow or tearing up a newspaper, simply aren't as effective anymore. If children have not yet developed self-control, they may learn that hitting when they are angry is OK, or they may be unable, once they start, to stop destroying other things. Instead, children can be redirected to a physical activity, such as running fast, or to a creative activity, such as working with clay, to channel their anger more constructively.[3]

USING THIS BOOK AT HOME WITH YOUR CHILD

1. Before reading the book to your child, talk together about situations or circumstances when you yourself have been angry. Ask your child: What makes *you* angry? When you are mad, what do you do?

2. Read the book to your child, looking at the illustrations and talking together about what is happening. Let your understanding of your child's interests and needs, as well as your child's own ideas and questions, guide the one-on-one conversation the two of you have. Talk about some of the following:

   - Have you ever been angry about something that made Simon angry here? What did you do?

   - If you were mad about something, what animal would you imagine might suddenly appear with you? How would it look? What do you think the animal would do?

   - Simon thought "it was great, it was marvelous, it was magical" to have a ferocious animal around to scare the people he was mad at. How do you think you would feel about having an animal like that around?

A GUIDE FOR PARENTS AND TEACHERS

BY MARTHA BETTIS GEE

One important developmental task of childhood is learning how to identify, express, and manage one's emotions. While this has always been a challenge for children and those who care about them, helping children deal with strong emotions such as anger is perhaps more challenging today than ever before. Here are two key factors that play a role in this:

1. **The Impact of Media.** In the past, parents had good reason to be concerned about violent content in television programming. But today the media our children can access goes far beyond the TV screen. Indeed, it is almost as pervasive as the air we breathe. With the increase in handheld and other portable devices, media exposure has moved beyond computers, TV, and the movies to content delivered through small screens not always easily monitored by parents or teachers. The 24/7 news cycle, with its instant updates on the day's breaking events, means that even very young children may see and hear accounts of violent events. When a child plays a violent video game or sees programming where adults act out their anger in impulsive, violent ways, is it any wonder that many teachers report that children are coming to child care or school with more anger and less self-control?[1]

2. **A Decline in the Civility of Public Discourse.** The ways in which adults interact, particularly around ideas where they disagree, seem to be markedly less civil these days. And when adults do disagree, the ways in which they express their differences are often, well, disagreeable. Even when it may seem that children do not notice what is going on, the chances are good that they see and hear and ultimately may replicate such behavior.

THE ROLE OF PARENTS AND TEACHERS

Parents and teachers understand that they have a key role in both modeling approaches and helping children learn strategies for channeling their emotions productively. Here are some things to keep in mind:

- **Acknowledge That Being Angry Is a Part of Being Human.** Sometimes what children learn from the way adults express their anger is that being angry is an unnatural response. A child may observe a parent who stiffens up or whose face and demeanor reveal some strong emotion but whose words are contradictory and confusing. At other times, children may witness angry outbursts directed by an adult to other drivers, or they may hear a parent explode at a bad call at a youth soccer game. When children observe adults having trouble putting words to their own anger, they may then have trouble naming their own emotions. When they experience the blowback from an adult's angry tirade that seems to come out of nowhere, they may become frightened or confused.

- **Model Appropriate Behavior.** Parents, teachers, and other adults in a child's life can model appropriate and healthy ways to deal with their own anger. When we are angry around children, whether or not the child's behavior is the source of our anger, we can strive to use words to express that anger. Sometimes it may be appropriate to say, "I am angry at you for what you just did." Sometimes you may

It was great, it was marvelous, it was magical to be calm, quiet, and peaceful. Everyone told him that his pretty butterflies were much nicer than the horrible dragon.

So Simon found a quiet spot to sit down. He closed his eyes and concentrated hard, until calm spread through his whole body. After a few moments, he felt as if his dragon had exploded into a thousand butterflies, each one carrying a little piece of his anger away.

He didn't know what
to do to get rid of his anger.
He tried shouting at it to make it go away,
but that only brought out worse creatures!